LETTERS FROM A PONY EXPRESS RIDER

SRA

Columbus, OH

SRAonline.com

 SRA

Send all inquiries to this address:
SRA/McGraw-Hill
4400 Easton Commons
Columbus, OH 43219

ISBN: 978-0-07-608776-1
MHID: 0-07-608776-X

2 3 4 5 6 7 8 9 NOR 13 12 11 10 09

The McGraw·Hill Companies

"George, you've been moping around all day," James said. "What's the matter?"

"I'm seventeen, and Pa doesn't treat me like a grown-up," George complained.

"Hey, I'm not a baby either—I'm eleven years old!" James said as he accidentally poured too much feed into the horses' trough.

"I know," George replied, "it's just that I so desperately want to head out West like all those families we see traveling through town. I want adventure and a challenge, so I think it's time for me to leave Missouri."

James dreaded the day his older brother would leave home, but he did not want George to know that.

The next afternoon James was practicing reading for his ma. Suddenly George burst through the door.

"Where's Pa?" he asked excitedly.

"What's so important?" asked Pa, walking into the house right behind him.

"I know you say I'm not ready to travel to the West on my own," George started, "but I saw this poster today that says they're looking for excellent horsemen like me to carry mail to the inhabitants in the West."

"I don't know. . ." Pa replied.

Ma joined their conversation, saying, "That's awfully dangerous territory."

James secretly hoped Pa would agree with her and refuse to let George go. He'd miss his brother too much.

Pa looked thoughtfully at George and said, "I've heard about the Pony Express. It starts in St. Joseph, not too far from here."

"What is it?" James asked.

"It's a system where a series of riders carry mail along a route from here to Sacramento, California," Pa said. "The people who moved to that territory need accurate information about what's going on out here. We might be headed for a civil war, and you'd be doing a tremendous service by carrying letters to them. But are you ready for the challenge of such a long trek?"

"I am!" George quickly responded.

James was not prepared to say good-bye to his brother.

The next day George and Pa went into town. There George registered with the Pony Express. He filled out the paperwork, answered lots of questions, and showed off his excellent riding skills. "The Pony Express is happy to have you," the man said as he shook George's hand. "We'll see you tomorrow."

At dinner George couldn't stop talking about the Pony Express and the adventures he would soon be having. James, on the other hand, was unusually quiet.

George sensed his brother's unhappiness. "You know, James, I'll be sure to write to you often, and you'll receive my letters by the Pony Express."

"Honest?" asked James.

"Yes," said George, "I'll leave letters along the route, and other riders will carry them back to Missouri. I'll correspond so often, it'll be like I never left."

James was aware that letters could never take his brother's place, but at least he'd have some kind of contact with him.

The following morning James helped George as he prepared to leave.

"I want you to have this," George said, handing a brown leather lasso to James.

"This is your favorite lasso," James said, "and you might need it."

"No, I won't, but you'd better take good care of it because I might want it back," George said, grinning.

James missed George's company right from the start.

He found that tending to the horses was much more difficult without his brother's help.

As he groomed the horses and filled their trough, James's mind often wandered to thoughts of his brother. He wondered where George was and what he was doing.

By the time several weeks had passed, James longed to receive one of those letters George had promised him. He was convinced it would never arrive.

Then one day James spotted Ma waving an envelope in the air.

He pestered her to open it immediately, so she ripped it open and read the letter aloud.

Dear Ma, Pa, and James,

I apologize for not writing sooner, but I've been riding day and night. I ride about a hundred miles at a time, stopping only at relay stations every ten miles or so for a fresh horse. Even then I'm allowed only two minutes to change horses!

About every hundred miles, I stop at home stations to eat and sleep, but then I'm off riding again.

The Pony Express keeps hundreds of horses, James. You'll be pleased to know they are well cared for. I always tell the other riders about you and the great care you give our horses back home.

Love,
George

James hurried to the stables as soon as Ma finished George's letter. He was determined to take good care of the horses. After all, George had bragged about him to everyone. He was sure to pay special attention to Old Mo, George's favorite horse.

James decided that riding Old Mo every day would make him feel closer to George. Each day he straddled the stallion and took off in a gallop. Whenever he saw Ma hanging the laundry, he would call out, "Look, Ma, I'm a rider on the Pony Express. I can't stop because I've got to get the mail to California!"

George's second letter arrived a few weeks later, and again Ma read it aloud:

Dear Pa, Ma, and James,
Winter is taking its toll. We used to get the mail to California in twelve days, but now it takes up to sixteen days. The freezing winds blow, and the snow makes traveling the rough terrain even harder than before, but our horses are amazing.

I pass many people on the Oregon Trail. I admire their determination to head for a better life. One family told me that they passed through Missouri and stocked up on supplies there. That really made me homesick.

Love,
George

James wondered if he had seen the family George mentioned in his letter. St. Joseph was a popular rest stop along the trek to the West, and every time James and Pa went into town, they met folks headed that way. Pa often helped them load supplies into their wagons.

James sometimes daydreamed about sneaking inside a wagon. He imagined catching up with George somewhere on the Pony Express route. Maybe he, too, could be a rider.

A couple of months later another letter arrived. This one was addressed only to him.

Dear James,

Don't let Ma read this because she'll only worry, but I had quite a surprise last night. I was galloping fast as lightning when my horse's hoof got caught up in an old prairie-dog hole! Those pesky critters dig burrows all over here. Fortunately my horse wasn't injured.

While I tended to him, I saw a lurking bandit in the shadows. He must have thought that I had money in my mochila, which is the leather pouch that holds the mail. I straddled my horse and skedaddled away from that thief as quickly as I could. He couldn't compete with my speed!

Love,
George

George continued to write whenever he could, sharing his adventures and often including some money he'd made. He sometimes earned as much as one hundred dollars a month!

In August, George's letter announced that he would be riding to St. Joseph and wanted to visit everybody. James couldn't wait to see his brother again.

When George galloped into the yard, James ran to him and hugged him.

"You're really skinny!" he said.

"You've grown a foot!" George replied.

James, George, and Pa headed straight to the stables.

"Old Mo and I ride every day," James said. "I'm training to ride the Pony Express!"

George was impressed with James's riding and said, "You're almost better than I am!"

"So I'm ready?" James asked.

"You're ready all right, but not necessarily for the Pony Express," George replied.

"Why not?" James retorted.

"It probably won't last much longer because the telegraph is set to take its place," Pa said. "That device uses wires and electricity to transmit messages."

"But I wanted to ride with George!" complained James.

"We may not be riding the Pony Express, but we'll surely be able to find something else to do together," George said, smiling. "With our skills, little brother, we can do anything!"

Vocabulary

trough (trôf) (page 3) *n.* A long narrow container that holds water or food for animals.

inhabitants (in ha´ bə tənts) (page 4) *n.* Plural of **inhabitant:** A person or animal that lives in a place.

accurate (ak´ yər it) (page 5) *adj.* Correct; exact.

registered (re´ jə stərd) (page 6) *v.* Past tense of **register:** To officially record.

longed (longd) (page 8) *v.* Past tense of **long:** To want very much; yearn.

straddled (stra´ dəld) (page 10) *v.* Past tense of **straddle:** To sit with one's legs on each side of an object.

lurking (lûr´ king) (page 13) *adj.* Lying hidden and quiet, preparing to attack.

Comprehension Focus: Predicting

1. George talks about working together with James. What do you predict they could do with their horse skills?

2. Do you predict George will want to stay in Missouri now that he has had a taste of the West? Why or why not?